This book belongs to _____.

Dick Bruna

Animal Book

Dick Bruna Books, Inc.
PRICE/STERN/SLOAN
Publishers, Inc., Los Angeles
1984

pig

sheep

COW

rooster

chicken

dog

duck

pigeon

snail

porcupine

rabbits

mouse

Books by Dick Bruna:

The Apple
The Little Bird
Lisa and Lynn
The Fish
Miffy
Miffy at the Zoo
Miffy in the Snow
Miffy at the Seaside
I Can Read
I Can Read More
A Story to Tell
I Can Count
Snuffy
Snuffy and the Fire
Miffy Goes Flying

Miffy's Birthday
I Can Count More
Animal Book
Miffy at the Playground
Miffy in the Hospital
Miffy's Dream
When I'm Big
I Know about Numbers
I Know More about Numbers
I Know about Shapes
Farmer John
Miffy's Bicycle
The Rescue
The Orchestra
Miffy Goes to School

First published in the U.S.A. 1984
by Dick Bruna Books Inc., New York
Illustrations Dick Bruna
Copyright Mercis bv., Amsterdam © 1972, all rights reserved
Text copyright © Dick Bruna 1984
Exclusively arranged and produced by Mercis Publishing bv., Amsterdam
Printed and bound by Brepols Fabrieken nv., Turnhout, Belgium
I.S.B.N. 0-8431-1575-0